Clifford's

CHRISTMAS WISHES

by Gail Herman
Illustrated by Mark Marderosian

Based on the Scholastic book series
"Clifford The Big Red Dog"
by Norman Bridwell

SCHOLASTIC INC.
New York   Toronto   London   Auckland   Sydney
Mexico City   New Delhi   Hong Kong   Buenos Aires

0-439-66763-1

15 14 13 12 11 10   14 15/0

Printed in the U.S.A.   40
First printing, November 2004

"Hooray!"

cheered Emily Elizabeth.

"It's Christmas Eve!

I love baking cookies."

"Hooray!"

cheered Clifford.

"It's Christmas Eve!

I love eating cookies."

"We're here to sing
Christmas carols!"
said Emily Elizabeth.

"No howling!"

Mr. Bleakman told Clifford.

But then he smiled.

"The Birdwell Island Christmas tree

is so beautiful every year,"

sighed Emily Elizabeth.

Clifford put the big star

on top.

Jetta and Mac walked by.

"Help us decorate the tree!"

called Emily Elizabeth.

Jetta looked sad.

"Not this Christmas," she said.

"What's wrong, Mac?"

Clifford hurried to catch up.

Mac didn't answer.

"Do you want to sneak treats

from Sheriff Lewis's kitchen?"

T-Bone asked.

Mac shook his head.

"How about putting more stuff

on the tree?" asked Cleo.

"Or singing more Christmas carols?"
asked Clifford.

He howled a few bars of "Jingle Bells."

Mac just looked sad.

"Let's have a Christmas party . . .

just for dogs!" said Clifford.

"We'll bring bones for gifts,

and make Christmas wishes!"

"I'm not making a silly wish!"

cried Mac.

"I'm not sharing my bones!

I don't like Christmas at all!"

He stormed away.

Clifford, T-Bone, and Cleo

followed Mac back to his house.

"Oh, Mac!" cried Jetta.

"I'm sorry I have to go away on Christmas."

"If only you could come," said Jetta.

"But you make my cousin sneeze.

I wish I could stay here with you!"

Clifford sighed.

No wonder Mac was sad!

Cleo nudged Clifford.

"Come on," she said.

"It's time for our party."

"Let's bring all our
Christmas bones to Mac,"
said Clifford.
"That will make him feel better!"

"Good idea!" said Cleo.

"But let's make our wishes first."

The dogs closed their eyes.

They each made a wish.

The dogs headed to Mac's house.

Clifford pulled his friends

and the bones

in a big wagon.

"It's snowing!" cheered T-Bone.

"A snowy Christmas!" said Cleo.

"My wish came true!"

"Merry Christmas, Mac!" said Clifford.

"These bones are all for you!

Now will you celebrate with us?"

"I guess we can share,"
said Mac with a shrug.
T-Bone scooped up a bone.
"My wish came true!"

Jetta ran outside.

"Mac! Mac!"

she shouted.

"This is a big snowstorm!" said Jetta.

"No one can leave the island.

I'm staying here with you!

My wish came true!"

"Did your wish come true?"

Cleo asked Clifford.

Clifford looked around.

Everyone was together.

Everyone was happy.

"Oh, yes,"

said Clifford.

"It did! Merry Christmas!"

Do You Remember?

Circle the right answer.

1. Who put the star on top of the Christmas tree?

    a. Charley

    b. Clifford

    c. Sheriff Lewis

2. What did T-Bone wish for?

    a. A snowy Christmas.

    b. Jetta and Mac to be together.

    c. A bone.

Which happened first?

Which happened next?

Which happened last?

Write a 1, 2, or 3 in the space after each sentence.

Mr. Bleakman told Clifford not to howl. _____

It started to snow. _____

Emily Elizabeth baked cookies. _____

Answers:

Emily Elizabeth baked cookies. (1)

It started to snow. (3)

Mr. Bleakman told Clifford not to howl. (2)

2. c

1. b